When the New Baby Comes, I'm Moving Out

STORY AND PICTURES BY

Martha Alexander

Dial Books for Young Readers / New York

Copyright © 1979 by Martha Alexander
All rights reserved.
Library of Congress Catalog Card Number: 79-4275
First Pied Piper Printing 1981
Printed in Hong Kong by South China Printing Co.
C O B E
6 8 10 9 7 5
A Pied Piper Book is a registered trademark of
Dial Books for Young Readers
® TM 1,163,686 and ® TM 1,054,312
WHEN THE NEW BABY COMES, I'M MOVING OUT
is published in a hardcover edition by
Dial Books for Young Readers
2 Park Avenue, New York, New York 10016
ISBN 0-8037-9563-7

For my
littlest grandson,
B.J.

"Why are you painting my old high chair?"

"I'm getting it ready for the new baby."

"The new baby! But that's *my* high chair.
And my crib—you're going to paint that too?

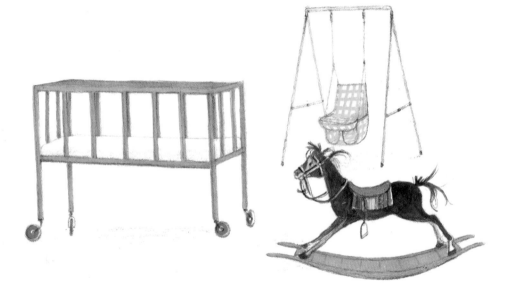

And all my old things!
You didn't even ask me.

I need those things! This was going to be
my spaceship launching pad.

And this is my cage for all my wild animals.
You can't give my cage away.

How would you like it if I gave
your bed away—or your rocking chair?"

"I'm sorry, Oliver. I didn't think
you wanted those old baby things."

"But I do want them—I *do.*
I need them. They're *mine.*

Look! You don't even have a lap anymore.
That baby is taking up all the room,
and it isn't even born yet.

I don't like you anymore.

I'm going to throw you in the garbage can!

And I'll put the lid on too.

And pound it with a stick.

And I won't give you any food.

I'll take you to the dump.
And I'll throw ashes on you.

I'll leave you there.
And you'll be sorry—both of you."

"What a terrible place to leave us—the dump!"

"Well, you could stay here if you want to,
and I'll leave.

I'll go live in my tree house.

Or maybe I'll camp in the woods—in my tent."

"I wish you wouldn't go away.
  I'd be so very sad and lonely without you."

"You would? You really would miss me?"

"Even more than that.
I'd be miserable without you.

Who would cut out the cookies
when I roll out the dough? And who
would play hide-and-seek with me?"

"I guess that baby won't be much fun
for you either. I better stay with you."

"You know, Oliver, big brothers get to do lots of very special things."

"They do?"

"You bet they do!"

"Hurry up, baby, I have lots of plans.
I can't wait to be a big brother."